Angus and Lucy didn't have very much,
but they had all they would ever need.

With bleary eyes and full hearts,
they rode through the clean morning air.

Nobody had said a word, but
Angus and Lucy knew exactly where they were going.

The next day, as the family yawned their good mornings,
they were closer than ever before.

one small home shone brighter than any other.

That night, as darkness fell upon the town,

They huddled beside the lamp
and listened to the story.

The light faded and the family moved inside,
Dad reading all the way.

Mum and Dad looked at the book. They opened it.
Dad read the first sentence aloud, then the second.

The children moved closer
as Dad turned the page and read on.

Then one afternoon,
something tumbled from Lucy's schoolbag.

'What's this?' said Dad.
'A book,' Lucy answered.
'From where?' asked Mum.
'The library,' Lucy replied.

there was a lot more space between them all.

And because there was more space in their home,

Angus couldn't reach the window.

But things were not the same.

Bowls slid off the table.

The books had to go.

their home could take no more.

Books cluttered every corner of their home,

until one day . . .

They were stacked here

and piled there,

balanced, propped and shoved
in all kinds of odd places.

hundreds of them.

But Angus and Lucy had books ...

They didn't even have a house.

They didn't have a car.

They didn't have a television.

Angus and Lucy didn't have very much.

# The children who loved books

PETER CARNAVAS

For Sophie and Elizabeth,
my favourite storytellers

First published in the UK in 2017
by New Frontier Publishing Europe Ltd.
93 Harbord Street, London SW6 6PN
www.newfrontierpublishing.co.uk

ISBN: 978-1-912076-18-5

A CIP catalogue record for this book is available from the British Library.

Printed in China
10 9 8 7 6 5 4 3 2 1

# The children who
# loved books